Frederick

Frederick

Leo Lionni

Dragonfly Books ⸺ New York

About the Author

Leo Lionni, an internationally known designer, illustrator, and graphic artist, was born in Holland and studied in Italy until he came to the United States in 1939. He was the recipient of the 1984 American Institute of Graphic Arts Gold Medal and was honored posthumously in 2007 with the Society of Illustrators Lifetime Achievement Award. His picture books are distinguished by their enduring moral themes, graphic simplicity, and brilliant use of collage, and include four Caldecott Honor Books: *Inch by Inch*, *Frederick*, *Swimmy*, and *Alexander and the Wind-Up Mouse*. Hailed as "a master of the simple fable" by the *Chicago Tribune*, he died in 1999 at the age of 89.

All rights reserved. Published in the United States by Dragonfly Books,
an imprint of Random House Children's Books, a division of Random House, Inc., New York.
Originally published in hardcover in the United States by Pantheon Books,
a division of Random House, Inc., New York, in 1967.

Dragonfly Books with the colophon is a registered trademark of Random House, Inc.

Visit us on the Web! www.randomhouse.com/kids

Educators and librarians, for a variety of teaching tools, visit us at www.randomhouse.com/teachers

The Library of Congress has cataloged the hardcover edition of this work as follows:
Lionni, Leo.
Frederick / by Leo Lionni.
Summary: Frederick the field mouse sat on the old stone wall while his four brothers gathered food
for the approaching winter days. The other mice felt that Frederick was not doing his share of the work,
but when the food ran out, Frederick saved the day with what he had gathered.
ISBN 978-0-394-81040-9 (hardcover) — ISBN 978-0-394-91040-6 (lib. bdg.) — ISBN 978-0-394-82614-1 (pbk.)
[1. Mice—Stories. 2. Picture books for children.]
I. Title.
PZ10.3.L6465 Fr5
[E]
72009556

MANUFACTURED IN CHINA
66 65 64 63 62 61 60 59 58

Frederick

All along the meadow where the cows grazed and the horses ran, there was an old stone wall.

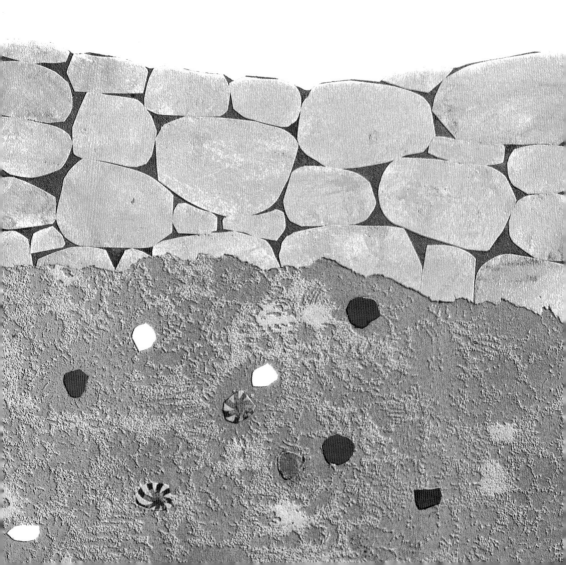

In that wall, not far from the barn and the granary,
a chatty family of field mice had their home.

But the farmers had moved away, the barn was abandoned, and the gran
stood empty. And since winter was not far off, the little mice began to ga
corn and nuts and wheat and straw. They all worked day and night.
All — except Frederick.

"Frederick, why don't you work?" they asked.
"I *do* work," said Frederick.
"I gather sun rays for the cold dark winter days."

And when they saw Frederick sitting there, staring at the meadow, they s.
"And now, Frederick?" "I gather colors," answered Frederick simply. "For
winter is gray."

And once Frederick seemed half asleep. "Are you dreaming, Frederick?" the asked reproachfully. But Frederick said, "Oh no, I am gathering words.
For the winter days are long and many,
and we'll run out of things to say."

The winter days came, and when the first snow fell
the five little field mice took to their hideout in the stones.

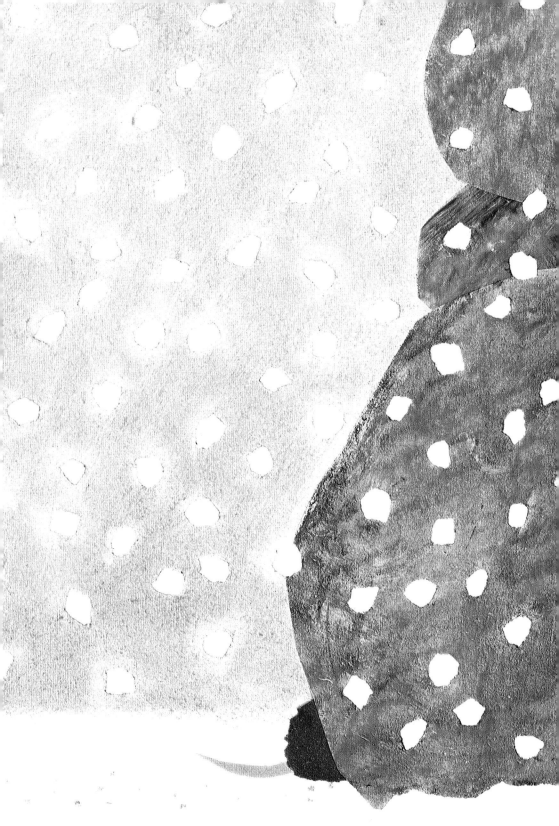

In the beginning there was lots to eat,
and the mice told stories of foolish foxes
and silly cats. They were a happy family.

But little by little they had nibbled up
most of the nuts and berries, the straw was
gone, and the corn was only a memory.
It was cold in the wall
and no one felt like chatting.

Then they remembered
what Frederick had said about sun rays
and colors and words.
"What about *your* supplies, Frederick?"
they asked.

"Close your eyes," said Frederick,
as he climbed on a big stone.
"Now I send you the rays of the sun.
Do you feel how their golden glow..."
And as Frederick spoke of the sun
the four little mice
began to feel warmer.
Was it Frederick's voice?
Was it magic?

"And how about the colors, Frederick?"
they asked anxiously. "Close your eyes again,"
Frederick said. And when he told them
of the blue periwinkles,
the red poppies in the yellow wheat,
and the green leaves
of the berry bush,
they saw the colors as clearly
as if they had been painted
in their minds.

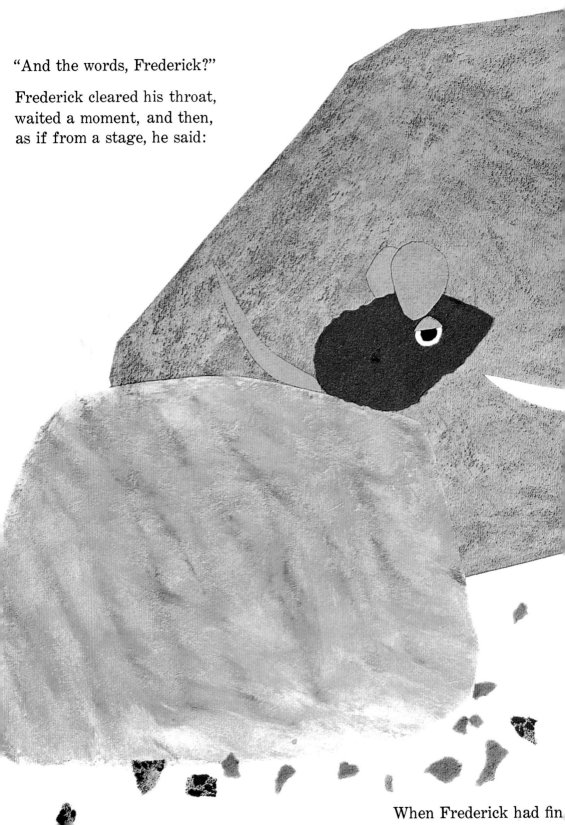

"And the words, Frederick?"

Frederick cleared his throat, waited a moment, and then, as if from a stage, he said:

When Frederick had fin

ho scatters snowflakes? Who melts the ice?
ho spoils the weather? Who makes it nice?
ho grows the four-leaf clovers in June?
ho dims the daylight? Who lights the moon?

ur little field mice who live in the sky.
ur little field mice . . . like you and I.

e is the Springmouse who turns on the showers.
en comes the Summer who paints in the flowers.
e Fallmouse is next with walnuts and wheat.
d Winter is last . . . with little cold feet.

en't we lucky the seasons are four?
ink of a year with one less . . . or one more!"

all applauded. "But Frederick," they said, "you are a poet!"

Frederick blushed, took a bow, and said shyly, "I know it."